KNOCK KNOCK
SUPERHERO

KNOCK KNOCK

Caryl Hart & Nick East

For Kat — you're Awesome! C.H.

**For Alfie & Basil,
two real super-dogs** N.E.

HODDER CHILDREN'S BOOKS

First published in Great Britain in 2020 by Hodder and Stoughton

Text © Caryl Hart, 2020
Illustrations © Nick East, 2020

The moral rights of the author and illustrator have been asserted.

A CIP catalogue record of this book
is available from the British Library.

HB ISBN: 978 1 444 94593 5
PB ISBN: 978 1 444 94594 2

10 9 8 7 6 5 4 3 2 1

Printed and bound in China.

 MIX
Paper from
responsible sources
FSC® C104740
www.fsc.org

Hodder Children's Books
An imprint of
Hachette Children's Group
Part of Hodder and Stoughton
Carmelite House
50 Victoria Embankment
London EC4Y 0DZ

An Hachette UK Company
www.hachette.co.uk

www.hachettechildrens.co.uk

Hodder
Children's
Books

KNOCK KNOCK
SUPERHERO

Caryl Hart & Nick East

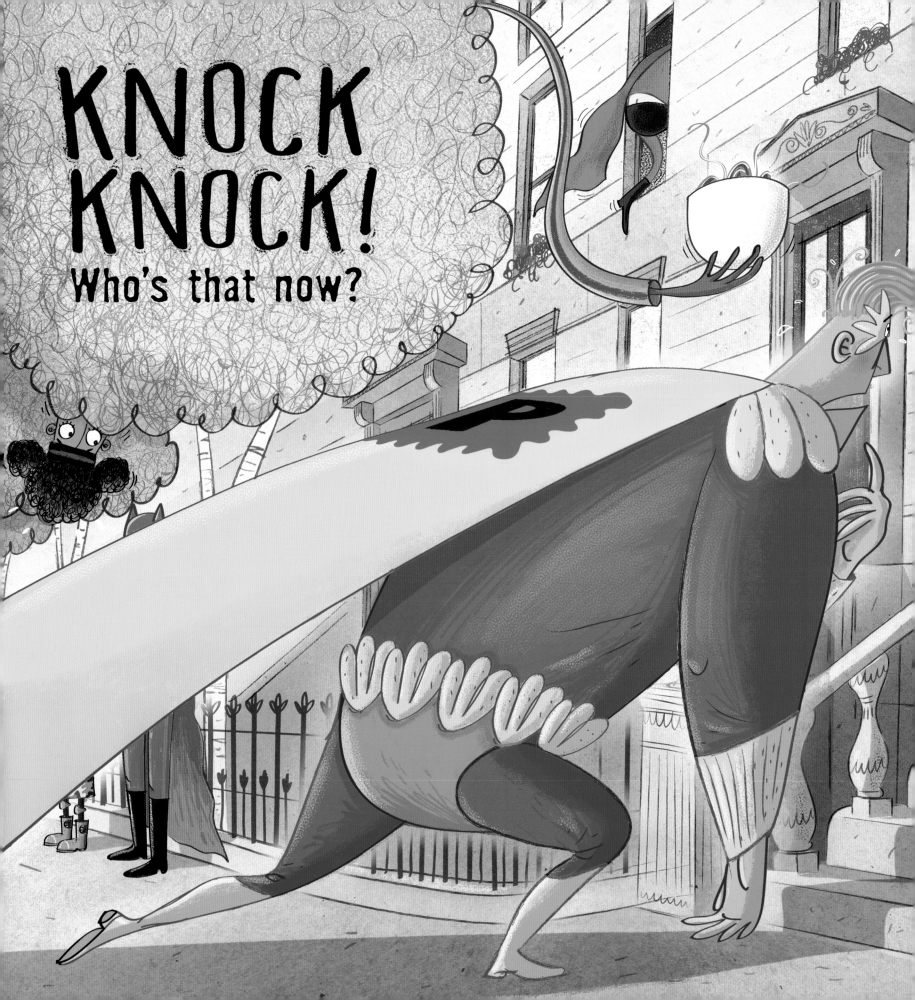

ONE superhero's outside. Wow!
"Quick! Let me in!" he begs me. "Please . . ."

"Is your name Pasta Man?" I say.
"Why are you at my house today?"
He groans, "It's not my finest hour.
I've run right out of Pasta Power!"

"That's sad," I shrug. "But I can't help."

Then Pasta Man lets out a yelp.
"Oh NO!" he cries. "I have to hide!"
He pushes past and runs inside.

Just then, TWO Muscle Mums appear.
"Quick! Madame Chilli's coming near!
She's out to rule the world by force
With lashings of hot chilli sauce!"

WHIZZZZZZZZZZ

ZIPPPPPPPP

THREE Glasses Girls all shout out, "Hey!
We saw you from six miles away.

We know exactly
what to do.
Quick! To the basement
— all of you!"

I see beside me
on the floor
A door that wasn't
there before.

The spiral stairs wind
round and round,
To a secret room,
deep underground . . .

"What IS this place?"
I gasp in awe.
"And what are all these
switches for?"

And there FOUR Gadget Grannies sit,
All testing gizmos while they knit.
"Oh, hello, dear! Put on your mask,
You'll need it for this dangerous task."

PHSSSSST

PHSSSST

"My babysitter's here," I say.
"He won't like 'dangerous'. No way!"

FIVE Brainy Boys laugh, "Don't be scared.
You'll be all right. We're well prepared."

So . . .

... we pull on capes
and flying boots,

magnetic gloves

and flame-proof suits.

"Come quick!" the Boys cry. "Here we are!
Our Supersonic Supercar!"
We all squash in. The switches glow.
"To Meatball Mountain! Off we go!"

But . . .

SIX Boo-hoo Babies fight and squeal
And try to grab the steering wheel.
They cry so much, they flood the cave.
"Watch out!" I yell. "A tidal wave!"

SWISH

SWOSH

The water churns.
The wipers swish.
I spot a whale, and lots of fish.
Then SEVEN Action Aunts swim by . . .

And lift our car into the sky!

SPLOSH

Just then I see a UFO.
It's Madame Chilli! Help! Oh no!
"HEY! Give me all your gadgets, guys!
I'm going to **rule the world!**"
she cries.

EIGHT Stretchy Stepdads, all fantastic,
Ping past on bright-pink pants elastic.
They whisk us off into the night.
"Look, Meatball Mountain's now in sight!"

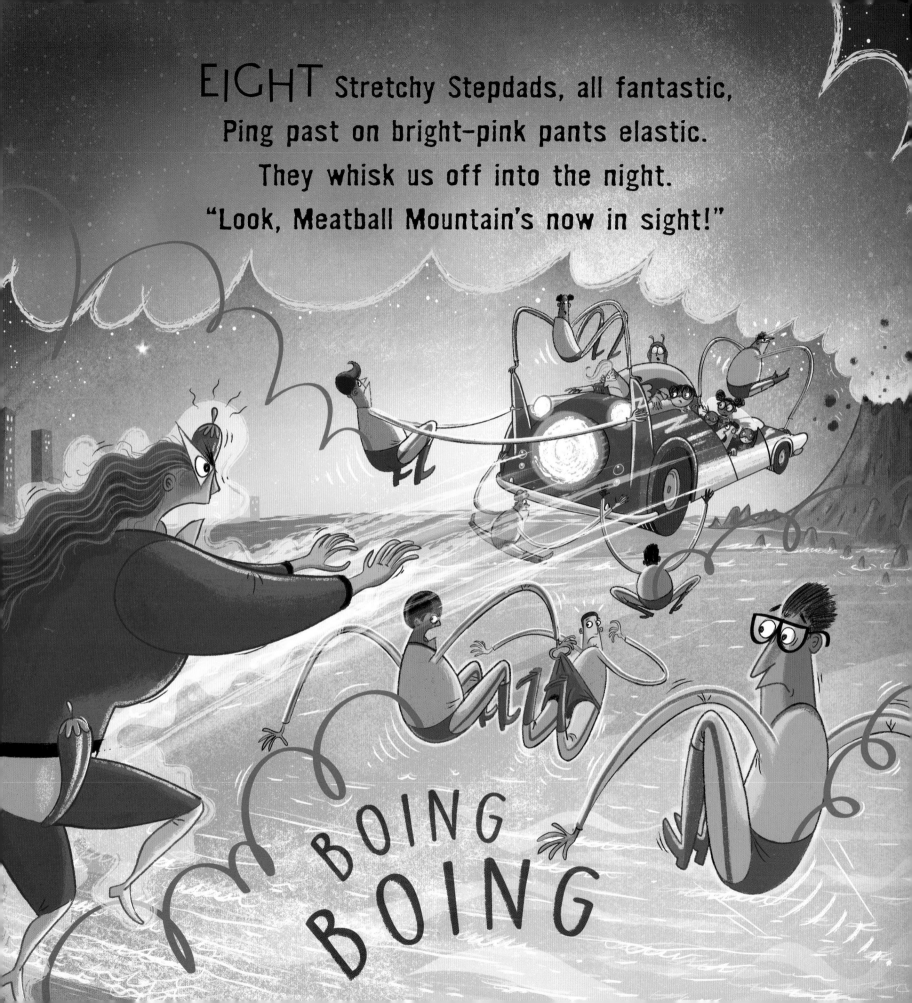

BOING
BOING

We park up on the crater's edge
Then inch along a narrow ledge,
Our faces lit up by the glow
Of bubbling Bolognese below.

Now Madame Chilli's closing in.

"Help! Pasta Man, don't let her win!"

But Pasta Man is tired and weak,

So feeble, he can hardly speak.

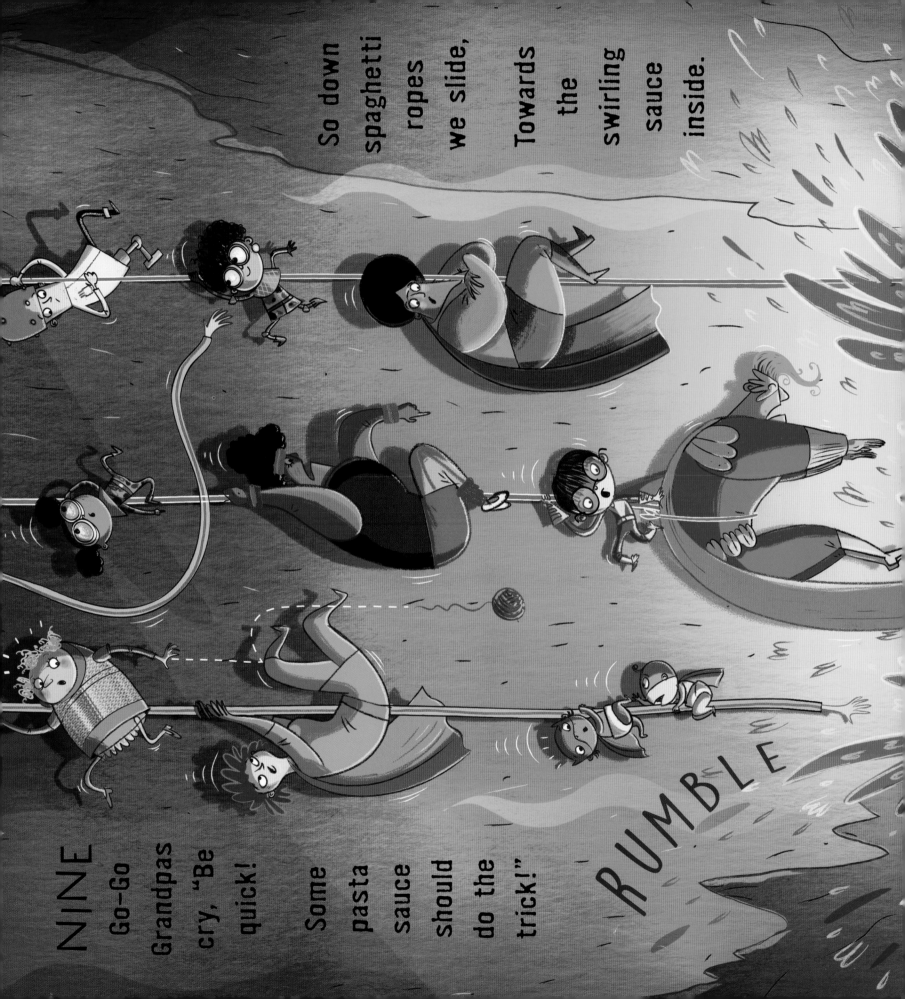

So down spaghetti ropes we slide,
Towards the swirling sauce inside.

NINE
Go-Go Grandpas cry, "Be quick!
Some pasta sauce should do the trick!"

RUMBLE

But as we reach the mountain's core
Huge cracks appear across the floor.
The mountain is erupting . . . oh!
It isn't safe! We have to go!

RUM
RUM

Yay! TEN Super Sisters swoop
And save us from the steaming gloop!
They catch our dinner on the way.
"Now, eat it while it's hot," they say.

SLURP

So Pasta Man eats up his food
And – look! – his Pasta Power's renewed.

He lassoes naughty Madame Chilli
And tells her off for being silly.

We fly home in no time at all
And when I climb up to the hall,
My babysitter smiles, "Hello!
Your supper's ready – here you go.

CREAK

Eat up and you'll be strong one day . . ."

"Oh, I already am!" I say.

To Lil, Sky and Son for putting up with my occasional grumpy feet,
and to everyone who woke up with grumpy feet this morning,
I hope you find your baby unicorn.
L.S.

First published in Great Britain in hardback 2016 by Boxer® Books Limited.
First published in Great Britain in paperback 2017 by Boxer® Books Limited.
www.boxerbooks.com
Boxer® is a registered trademark of Boxer Books Limited.

Text and illustrations copyright © 2016 Lisa Stubbs

The right of Lisa Stubbs to be identified as the author and
illustrator of this work has been asserted by her
in accordance with the Copyright, Designs and Patents Act, 1988.

The illustrations were screen printed by the author.
The text is set in Goudy Old Style.

ISBN 978-1-910716-06-9

1 3 5 7 9 10 8 6 4 2

Printed in China

This Bngs to

. . . .

love your library

Buckinghamshire Libraries

Search, renew or reserve online 24/7
www.buckscc.gov.uk/libraries

24 hour renewal line
0303 123 0035

Enquiries
01296 382415

follow us **twitter**
@Bucks_Libraries

Lily and Bear
Grumpy Feet

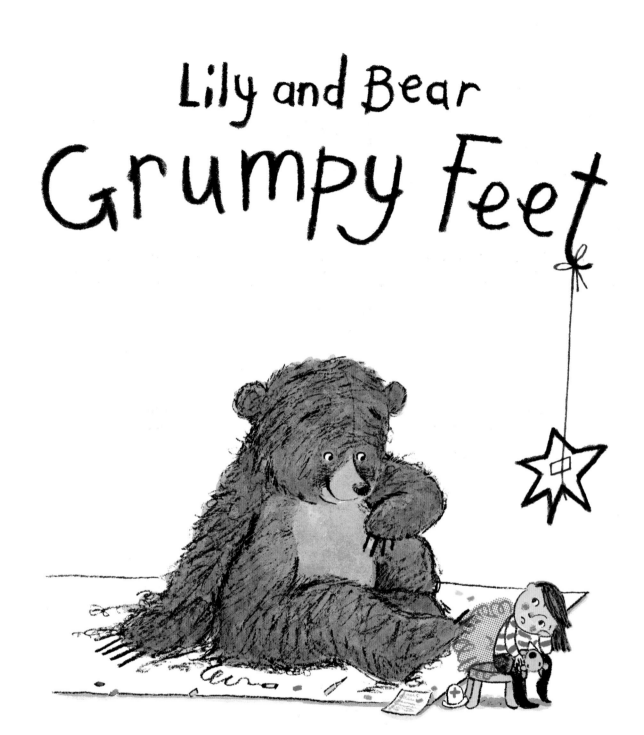

Lisa Stubbs

Boxer Books

Lily loved to draw,
but today something
felt different.

Things felt a little frumpy
and bumpy, just not so and
not quite right.

The day was
too rainy,

the teapot was
too dribbly
and the sunshine
colour was missing.

Lily's pencils were
too pointy,

her paint
too sloshy

and her crayons
too stubby.

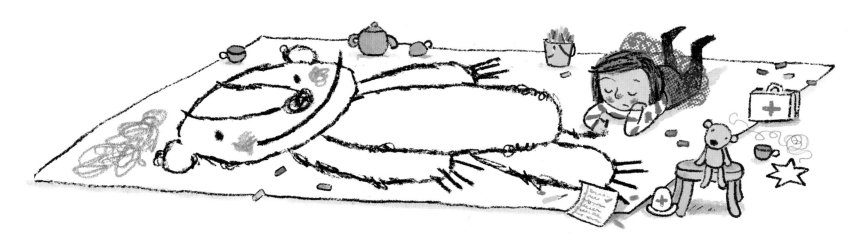

Everything felt grouchy and mouchy,
out of sorts and discombobbled.

Things to do...
1. Draw bear ✓
2. Drive to the moon
3. ~~drink~~ drink hot chocolate
4. polish stars
5. Jump really very high
6. find a baby unicorn

Until she drew . . .

Bear!

Bear put on his doctor's hat
and stethoscope and listened . . .

It was clear to Bear what was wrong . . .

Lily had

grumpy feet!

Bear thought it would help
if Lily wore happy shoes . . .

But things still felt frumpy and bumpy, just not so and not quite right.

Lily's feet were still grumpy.

Bear thought
it might help
if Lily had some
sticky cake.

But Lily's feet were
still grumpy.

Lily took her grumpy feet
to sit in the toy box.

Bear looked at Lily's list and
had a marvellous idea.

He set to work immediately . . .

Bear squeezed into the
toy box next to Lily
and started the engine.
"Where are we going?"
asked Lily.

Bear drove past the
rainy day, dribbly
teapot and missing
sunshine colour.

Past the pointy pencils,
sloshy paint and
stubby crayons.

Past the happy shoes
and sticky fishy cake.

"To a place that glows all comfy, not frumpy and bumpy. It is very so and just right," said Bear, as they drove into the starry night.

They drank hot chocolate and polished the stars. Then Bear played a happy moon tune on his banjo.

Lily's feet started
to tap and smile.

Lily's feet started
to wiggle and giggle.

Lily's feet started
to laugh and jump . . .   really very high!

Bear had turned the grumps
into the jumps!
There was only one thing left to do.

Number 6 on Lily's list.

Find a baby unicorn . . .

And they did.

More Boxer Books for you to enjoy

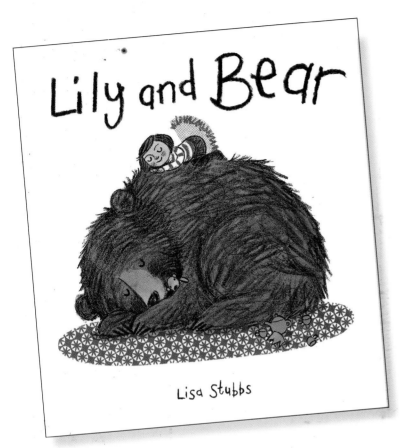

Lily and Bear

by Lisa Stubbs

Lily loves Bear and Bear loves Lily. They are the best of friends – and being best friends means taking turns. So some of the day they do Lily things and some of the day they do Bear things.

A truly magical story about the give and take of friendship.

Croc? What Croc?

by Sam Williams

Illustrated by Cecilia Johansson

Join Little Fluff on his stroll through the jungle, meeting his friends along the way. But why are they all shouting "Croc!"?

A fun, read-aloud story with rhythm and repetition that little ones will want to chant along to.

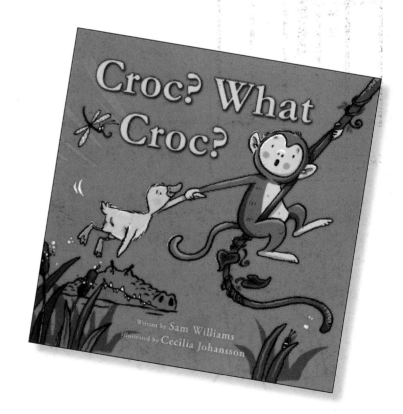

www.boxerbooks.com